MY LITTLE BOOK ABOUT
THE FLOPSY BUNNIES

NEW SEASONS
PUBLISHING

Copyright © 1991 Publications International, Ltd.
ISBN 1-56173-132-3
Based on the original story by Beatrix Potter
with all new illustrations
Cover illustration by Anita Nelson
Book illustration by Nan Brooks
Contributing editor: Barbara Armstrong Schwartz

When Benjamin Bunny grew up he married Flopsy, Peter Rabbit's sister. They had such a large family that everyone just called them the "Flopsy Bunnies."

Because there was not always enough to eat, Benjamin used to borrow cabbages from Peter Rabbit, who had a vegetable garden. But sometimes Peter Rabbit had no cabbages to spare. When this happened, the Flopsy Bunnies went across the field to a trash pile in the ditch outside Mr. McGregor's garden.

Mr. McGregor's trash pile was a jumble of jars and paper bags, oily-tasting grass clippings, rotten vegetables, and an old boot or two. One day—oh joy!—there was overgrown lettuce, which had gone to flower.

Benjamin and his Flopsy Bunny children stuffed themselves with the lettuce leaves. With their tummies full, the bunnies grew sleepy and lay down in the soft grass clippings. Before going to sleep, Benjamin slipped a paper bag over his head to keep the flies from bothering him.

The little Flopsy Bunnies slept soundly in the warm sun. From the lawn beyond the garden came the faraway hum of Mr. McGregor's lawn mower. The blue-bottle flies buzzed about the wall, and a little old mouse named Thomasina Tittlemouse picked over the trash pile. She rustled across the paper bag and woke Benjamin Bunny.

While Thomasina and Benjamin were chatting, they heard the steps of heavy boots. Suddenly, Mr. McGregor emptied a sackful of grass clippings right on top of the sleeping Flopsy Bunnies! Benjamin hid under his paper bag and Thomasina Tittlemouse crept inside a jar.

The little bunnies smiled sweetly in their sleep. They did not wake up in the shower of grass. They dreamed their mother was tucking them into their beds.

Mr. McGregor looked down after emptying his sack. He saw the tips of some furry little ears sticking up through the grass clippings. He stared at the little ears for a long time.

Then a fly settled on one of the ears. And the ear twitched.

Mr. McGregor pulled his chair from the table and sat down. The Flopsy Bunnies heard him chuckle, "One, two, three, four, five, six little rabbits!"

"Eh? What's that?" asked Mrs. McGregor. "What have the rabbits been spoiling now?"

Mr. McGregor only repeated, "One, two, three, four, five, six little fat rabbits!"

"Don't be a silly old man," scolded Mrs. McGregor. "Tell me what you mean!"

"In the sack!" Mr. McGregor pointed to the lumpy sack on the table. "Six little rabbits for supper!"

Mr. McGregor climbed down onto the trash pile. "One, two, three, four, five, six little rabbits for supper!" he said, as he put the sleeping bunnies into his sack. The Flopsy Bunnies dreamed their mother was turning them over in their beds. They still did not wake up.

Mr. McGregor tied the sack with string and left it on the garden wall while he put away his lawn mower.

While he was gone, Mrs. Flopsy Bunny came across the field. She looked at the sack sitting on the garden wall. She wondered where Benjamin and her children were. Thomasina Tittlemouse came out of her jar and Benjamin took the paper bag from his head. They told Flopsy the sad tale.

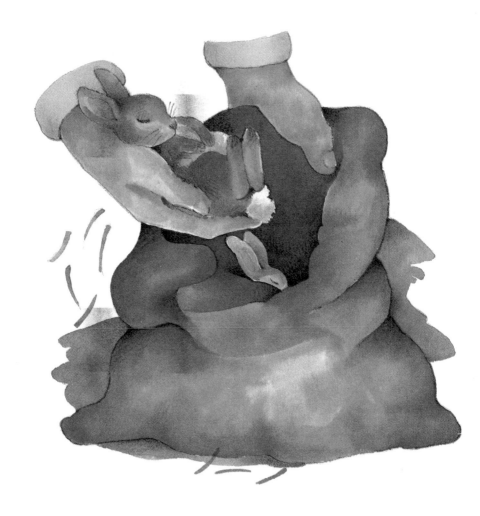

Benjamin and Flopsy were without hope. They could not untie the string that bound the sack. What could be done?

Mrs. Tittlemouse was a very clever mouse. She nibbled a hole in the bottom corner of the sack! The little bunnies were pulled out and awakened. Benjamin and Flopsy then filled the sack with three rotten squashes, an old boot brush, and two overly ripe turnips. Then they all hid under a bush and watched for Mr. McGregor.

After a while, Mr. McGregor came back. He picked up the sack and carried it off. The Flopsy Bunnies followed at a safe distance. They watched him go into his house. They crept to the window to watch and listen.

Mrs. McGregor felt the sack. "They must be *old* rabbits. They are hard and are all different shapes." She untied the sack and reached inside.

When she found the rotten vegetables and old boot brush she grew angry. She was sure Mr. McGregor had tried to trick her. She did not like his idea of a joke one little bit!

Mr. McGregor was angry, too. He threw one of the squashes right out the kitchen window. He just missed hitting the youngest Flopsy Bunny who had been watching from the windowsill!

Benjamin and Flopsy decided it was time to go home.

That Christmas Thomasina Tittlemouse was given a very lovely gift. The grateful Flopsy Bunnies presented her with enough soft rabbit fur to make herself a coat, a hood, a handsome muff, and a pair of warm mittens.